First published 1984
Published by Hamish Hamilton Children's Books
Garden House 57–59 Long Acre London WC2E 9JZ
Copyright © 1984 by Martin Bridle and Su Eaton
All Rights Reserved

British Library Cataloguing in Publication Data
Bridle, Martin
1. Title
2. Eaton, Su
823'.914 [J]   PZ7
ISBN 0-241-11222-2
Typeset by Katerprint Co Ltd, Oxford
Printed in Belgium by Henri Proost

Punch and Judy in the Rain

by Su Eaton and Martin Bridle

Hamish Hamilton · London

It is raining at the seaside, and everyone is cold and wet. The donkeys are being taken home and the ice cream man is shutting his stall.

The wind whistles and the raindrops splash. But
what is that noise? It sounds like someone snoring.
It is coming from the Punch and Judy booth.

It *is* someone snoring. It's old Mister Punch. He is fast asleep and probably dreaming. He doesn't care about the rain. He smiles and snores through it all.

Hey, wake up Mister Punch! May we come in? We're getting soaked out here!

"Well, how do you do? And how are you? Come in, come in."

It's dry in here with not much happening. There is Punch's Dog Toby asleep in his basket.

Look, there is a door under the cobwebs in the corner.
"We'll see all my friends down here," says Punch. "They are waiting until it is time for the next show to begin."

This is Punch's bedroom. What a lot of stripes!
Come and see the rest of the house.

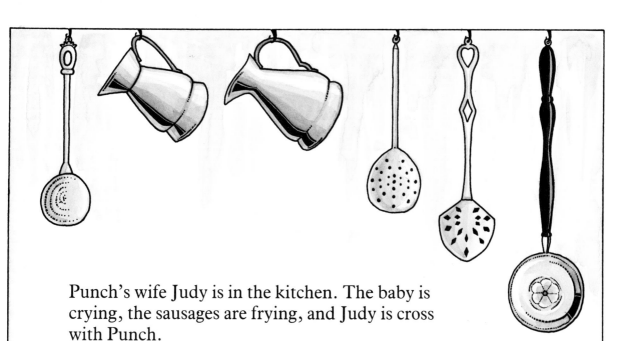

Punch's wife Judy is in the kitchen. The baby is crying, the sausages are frying, and Judy is cross with Punch.

"I don't have time for visitors," complains Judy.
"Who is going to look after the baby?"
"Out of my kitchen, Toby, and take Punch with you."

This is the cottage where Jack Ketch the Hangman lives. He his trying out his new invention. What is it? "It's a sausage machine," Jack says. "I have to make lots of sausages to keep the crocodile happy. We wouldn't want him to go hungry, now would we?"

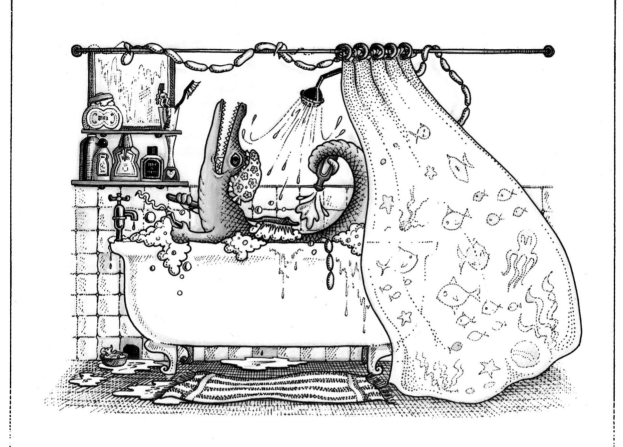

The happy, snappy crocodile is in the bath polishing his scales.

"See you later," says Jack.
"Not if I can help it!" says Punch.

Here is the policeman huffing and puffing on his bicycle. "I hope you're keeping out of mischief, Mr Punch," he says. "Do you have a licence for that dog?"

Look, old Joey the Clown is practising his plate-spinning act.
"Whoops, that's enough of that," laughs Joey.
"Let's have some music now."

That's the way to do it!

Now it is time to visit the last room in Punch's house
– the cellar!
"Look out behind you, Mister Punch!"
But he doesn't see anything.

"Well, that's all," says Punch, "unless you'd like a peep down below . . .?"
Yes please.
"Alright, but only if you're sure. You are sure, aren't you?"
Yes we're sure.
"Alright then, here we go . . . DOWN BELOW!"

Oh my! It's the Devil and the Bogeyman going about their wicked business. Toby has dropped his bone and it has landed on the Devil's head! Quick, let's get out of here!

"I'll get even with you," shouts the Devil.

Upstairs we go as fast as we can, through
all the rooms into Punch's bedroom.
Quick, hide!

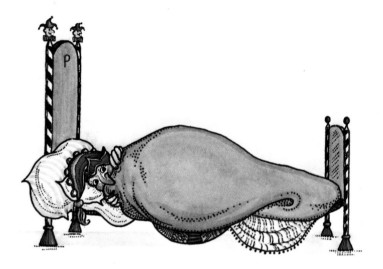

The next thing he knows, the sun is
shining through his window and there is
a shout from outside.
"Wake up, Mister Punch, wake up!"
The children are waiting for the show to
begin.

In no time at all, Punch is up on stage.
He opens the curtains and begins
everybody's favourite show.
"Ladies and Gentlemen, how do you do,
how do you do, and how do you do
again?"